LIONEL·AT·LARGE

LIONEL
·AT·
LARGE

by Stephen Krensky
pictures by Susanna Natti

PUFFIN BOOKS

For Joan
S.K.

For Jonathan and Anna
S.N.

PUFFIN BOOKS
Published by the Penguin Group
Penguin Books USA Inc., 375 Hudson Street, New York, New York 10014, U.S.A.
Penguin Books Ltd, 27 Wrights Lane, London W8 5TZ, England
Penguin Books Australia Ltd, Ringwood, Victoria, Australia
Penguin Books Canada Ltd, 10 Alcorn Avenue, Toronto, Ontario, Canada M4V 3B2
Penguin Books (N.Z.) Ltd, 182–190 Wairau Road, Auckland 10, New Zealand

Penguin Books Ltd, Registered Offices: Harmondsworth, Middlesex, England

First published in the United States of America by Dial Books for Young Readers, 1986
First paperback edition published by Dial Books for Young Readers, 1988
Published in a Puffin Easy-to-Read edition, 1993

1 3 5 7 9 10 8 6 4 2

LIBRARY OF CONGRESS CATALOGING-IN-PUBLICATION DATA
Krensky, Stephen.
Lionel at large / by Stephen Krensky;
pictures by Susanna Natti.   p.   cm. — (Puffin easy-to-read)
"Reading level 2.0" — T.p. verso.
"First published in the United States of America by Dial Books
for Young Readers, 1986"—T.p. verso.
Summary: Lionel faces such ordeals as having to eat green beans,
going to the doctor, and looking for the snake his sister lost in his room.
ISBN 0-14-036542-7
[1. Family life—Fiction.]
I. Natti, Susanna, ill. II. Title. III. Series.
[PZ7.K883Lj 1993]
[E]—dc20   93-6550   CIP   AC

Puffin® and Easy-to-Read® are registered trademarks of Penguin Books USA Inc.
Printed in the United States of America

Reading Level 2.0

CONTENTS

Vegetables ▪ 7

At the Doctor's ▪ 17

The Snake ▪ 27

The Baby ▪ 35

The Sleepover ▪ 45

VEGETABLES

Lionel and his family

were eating dinner.

They were having hamburgers.

Lionel liked to eat around

the edge of his roll

before biting into the middle.

The middle was covered with ketchup.

"Wipe your face, Lionel,"

said Mother.

"It's covered with ketchup."

Lionel used his napkin.

"What about Louise?" he asked.

His big sister smiled at him.

"My face is clean," said Louise.

"I never make a mess at the table."

She carefully ate a green bean.

It was her last one.

Lionel's plate was still full

of green beans.

He stared at them.

"Eat your vegetables, Lionel,"

said Father.

His father always ate everything.

"There's no room for them,"
said Lionel.

"You had room for your hamburger,"
said Mother.

She always ate everything too.

"That was different," said Lionel.

"Oh?" said Mother.

Lionel looked down at his stomach.

"I have shelves in here,"
he explained.

"They hold the food I eat."

Lionel felt one rib.

"Here is my hamburger shelf," he said.

Lionel felt another rib.

"Here is my bread shelf," he said.

"What about your vegetable shelf?"
asked Father.

Lionel felt both sides.

"I don't have one," he said.

"Hmmmph!" said Louise.

"If Lionel says he doesn't have
a vegetable shelf," said Father,
"I believe him."

"So do I," said Mother. "And we
can't expect him to eat his vegetables
if he has no place to put them."

Lionel smiled.

"Time for dessert," said Mother.

"Hooray!" said Lionel.

"Too bad you can't have any, Lionel," said Father.

"What do you mean?" Lionel asked.

"I've read a lot about
these shelves," said Father.
"The books say that
if you have no vegetable shelf,
you have no dessert shelf either."
"Hooray!" said Louise.
"Now there will be more for me."
Lionel felt his ribs again.

14

"Wait!" he shouted. "I think

I found my vegetable shelf.

It was hidden under the bread shelf."

He began eating his beans.

"See," he said. "I was right."

"How lucky," said Father.

"That was a close call,"

said Mother.

Lionel thought so too.

AT THE DOCTOR'S

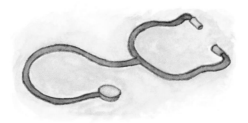

Lionel's mother walked into
the doctor's waiting room.
Lionel was supposed to be
right behind her.
He was still out in the hall.
"Come on, Lionel," said Mother.
"It's just a checkup."

Lionel did not like checkups.

He sat with his mother

until his name was called.

Then they went into

the doctor's office.

The doctor smiled at Lionel.

Lionel did not smile back.

"Please sit down," said the doctor.

Lionel sat.

"Stick out your tongue,"

said the doctor.

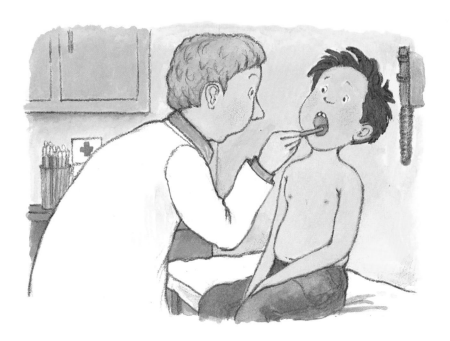

Lionel stuck out his tongue.

He took deep breaths while the doctor
listened to his chest.

Lionel did everything he was told.

"May I go now?" asked Lionel.

"Not yet," said the doctor.

"I have to give you a shot."

"Are you sure?" asked Lionel.

"I'm sure," said the doctor.

Lionel was afraid of that.

He hated shots.

He hated bee stings too.

But a shot was worse

because he knew when it was coming.

He closed his eyes
and wrinkled his nose.
"Just a minute," said the doctor.

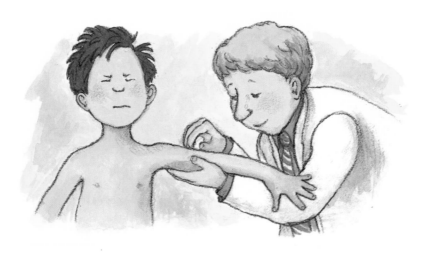

He brushed Lionel's arm with cotton.
"One more second," said the doctor.
"I have to take aim."
Lionel felt a prick in his arm.
"Are you ready?" asked the doctor.

Lionel clenched his teeth.

Nothing happened.

"All done," said the doctor.

Lionel opened one eye.

He opened the other too.

"I didn't feel anything," said Lionel.

"Really?" said his mother.

"You were very brave,"

said the doctor.

Lionel looked at him.

"You gave me the shot

while you were aiming."

"That's true," said the doctor.

"Did you mind?"

Lionel wanted to mind, but he couldn't.

He was glad the shot hadn't hurt.

The doctor gave Lionel a lollipop.

"Next time you'll need a new trick,"

said Lionel.

"Yes," said the doctor. "I guess I will."

"Don't forget," said Lionel.

Then he took his lollipop

and went home.

THE SNAKE

Louise was standing in Lionel's room.

She was holding an empty shoebox.

There were holes in the lid.

Lionel walked in.

"Don't move," said Louise.

"It's my room," said Lionel.

"I can move if I want to."

"Okay," said Louise.

"But don't step on my snake.

I dropped it on the floor."

Lionel jumped. He hated snakes.

"Where did it go?" he asked.

"I'm not sure," said Louise.

This is terrible, thought Lionel.

The snake could be anywhere.

It could be inside his dresser,

sleeping in a sock.

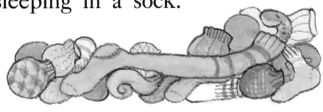

It could be in his bed,

curled up under his pillow.

It could be in his toy box,

stretched out on his electric train.

"We'll have to find it," said Louise.

"I'll look under the bed.

You look in the closet."

Lionel froze.

He did not want to look in the closet.

A closet was just the sort of place

a snake would go.

It was dark and warm

like a hole in the ground.

If he were a snake,

he would like a closet.

Lionel stared at the closet door.

He might never open it again.

Never.

But then he remembered something.

His baseball glove was in the closet.

His best shirt was in there too.

No snake was going to slither

all over his stuff

and get away with it.

"Go find your own baseball glove,
snake!" he shouted.

Lionel threw open the closet door.

He saw all of his favorite things.

But he did not see the snake.

"I've got him!" shouted Louise.

"He was under the radiator."

She stood up, holding the snake.

"Do you want to pet him?"

"I don't think so," said Lionel.

"He's had enough excitement

for one day."

THE BABY

The backyard was filled with

building sounds.

Lionel was cutting wood with a saw.

Zip-zaw, zip-zaw, zip-zaw.

His friend Jeffrey

was hammering nails into the wood.

Bang, bang, bang, bang.

Louise came out the back door.

"Guess what we're making?"

said Lionel.

"You're making a lot of noise,"

said Louise.

"My mother is going to have a baby,"

said Jeffrey.

"We're making the baby a sandbox."

Louise looked at the pieces of wood.

"It will be a very small sandbox,"
she said.

"It will be a very small baby,"
said Lionel.

"A baby brother," said Jeffrey.

Louise made a face.

"Sisters are better," she said.

"All baby brothers ever do
is eat and cry."

"They do not!" said Lionel.

"You don't even remember,"
said Louise. "I do."

She walked away.

Lionel frowned.

He could remember

making a snowman last winter.

He could remember

swimming at the beach last summer.

But he couldn't remember

being a baby.

What if he really did

eat and cry all the time?

"This baby could be

a lot of trouble," said Jeffrey.

He put down his saw.

Lionel put down his hammer.

"My father will remember," he said.

"Let's go ask him."

Lionel's father was raking leaves.

"How's the project coming?" he asked.

"Louise says brothers

make awful babies," said Jeffrey.

"She said Lionel just ate and cried

all the time."

"Is that true?" Lionel asked.

His father smiled.

"You did eat and cry a lot," he said.

"But that's what babies do best."

"Both girl and boy babies?"

asked Lionel.

His father nodded.

"As I recall," he said, "Louise

was very hungry and noisy too."

Lionel beamed.

"It sounds like babies are a lot
of trouble," said Jeffrey.

"Yes," said Father. "But they're worth it."
Jeffrey was glad of that.

He didn't want to have
all that trouble for nothing.

"Come on, Lionel," said Jeffrey.

"We have work to do."

And they ran off to finish
the sandbox.

THE SLEEPOVER

Lionel and his mother

were driving to Jeffrey's house.

Lionel was going to sleep over there.

"We're here!" shouted Lionel.

His mother stopped the car.

"May I have a kiss good-bye?"

Mother asked.

"No," said Lionel.

"I'm too old for good-bye kisses."

He got out of the car.

"Good-bye," said Mother.

"I'll see you tomorrow."

"Good-bye," said Lionel.

His mother drove away.

Jeffrey and Lionel

were explorers all afternoon.

Jeffrey found a lake.

"This is Lake Jeffrey,"

he said.

Lionel found a mountain.

"This is Lionel Mountain,"

he said.

They ate a big dinner
with Jeffrey's parents.
After dinner Lionel and Jeffrey
climbed into the spaceship
Jeffrey kept in the backyard.
Then they flew to the moon.

"It's getting late," said Jeffrey.

"And we have a long flight back,"
said Lionel.

They flew home in time to go to bed.

Jeffrey's parents came in

to say good night.

After they left

Jeffrey and Lionel lay in the dark.

"What should we do tomorrow?"

asked Lionel.

"Should we explore under

the sea?"

Jeffrey did not answer.

He was asleep.

Lionel stared at the ceiling.

He couldn't sleep.

The bed was soft,

but it wasn't his bed.

The pillow was fluffy,

but it wasn't his pillow.

He missed having the light
on in the hall.
He even missed hearing Louise
sing along with the radio.
Most of all,
he missed his mother's good night kiss.

Lionel finally got out of bed.

He went downstairs

and called home.

"Hello," said Mother.

"Hello," said Lionel.

"This is Lionel."

"Hello, Lionel," said Mother.

"You're up very late."

"I wanted to make sure

everyone was all right," he said.

"Father is asleep," said Mother.

"And Louise?" asked Lionel.

"Louise is asleep too," said Mother.

"But you're not," said Lionel.

"I couldn't sleep," said Mother.

"I missed giving you a good night kiss."

"Oh," said Lionel.

"Would you mind if I give you a good night kiss over the phone?" asked Mother.

"I don't mind," said Lionel.

Mother blew him a kiss.

"Why don't you go to sleep now?" she said. "Good night, Lionel."

"Good night," said Lionel.

He hung up the phone

and went back to bed.

Lionel was glad he had called home.

The bed felt softer.

The pillow felt fluffier.

Lionel's eyes slowly closed.

And soon he was fast asleep.